COSTUME QUEST:

INVASION OF THE CANDY SNATCHERS

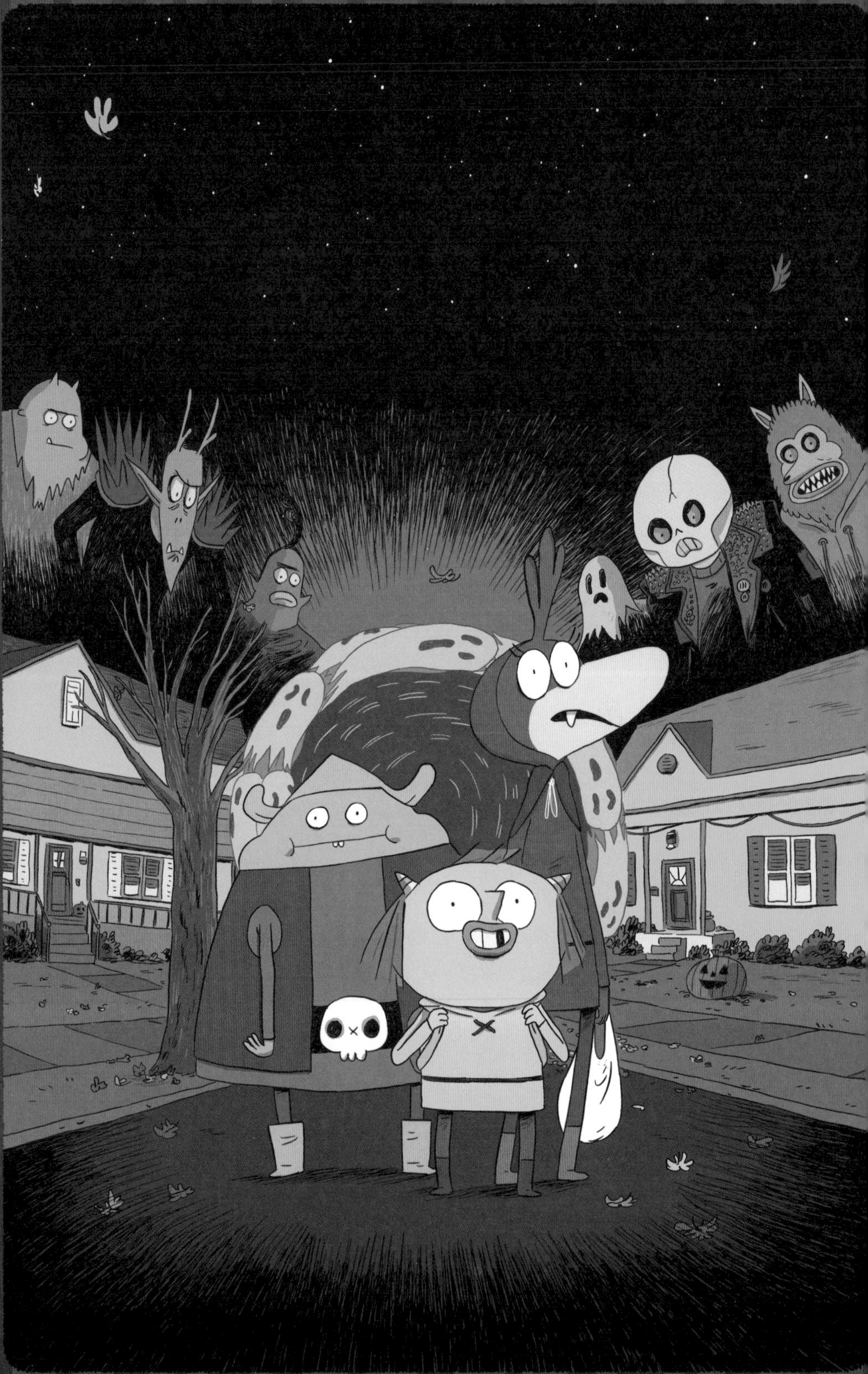

Costume Quest:

INVASION OF THE CANDY SNATCHERS

By
Zac Gorman

Based on the *Costume Quest* world created by
Tasha Sounart and Double Fine Productions

Designed by
Keith Wood

Edited by
Charlie Chu

Published by Oni Press, Inc.
Joe Nozemack, founder & chief financial officer
James Lucas Jones, publisher
Charlie Chu, v.p. of creative & business development
Brad Rooks, director of operations
Melissa Meszaros, director of publicity
Margot Wood, director of sales
Sandy Tanaka, marketing design manager
Amber O'Neill, special projects manager
Troy Look, director of design & production
Hilary Thompson, senior graphic designer
Kate Z. Stone, graphic designer
Sonja Synak, junior graphic designer
Angie Knowles, digital prepress lead
Ari Yarwood, executive editor
Sarah Gaydos, editorial director of licensed publishing
Robin Herrera, senior editor
Desiree Wilson, associate editor
Alissa Sallah, administrative assistant
Jung Lee, logistics associate
Scott Sharkey, warehouse assistant

Oni Press, Inc.
1319 SE Martin Luther King Jr. Blvd.
Suite 240
Portland, OR 97214
USA

onipress.com • facebook.com/onipress • @onipress • onipress.tumblr.com

doublefine.com • @doublefine

magicalgametime.com • zacgorman.com • @zacgormania

First edition: October 2014
Softcover edition: September 2018

ISBN 978-1-62010-559-7
eISBN 978-1-62010-191-9

Library of Congress Control Number: 2018938813

10 9 8 7 6 5 4 3 2 1

PRINTED IN CHINA.

For my mom, for making my Halloween costumes,
and my dad, for taking me to the comic store.

– Zac

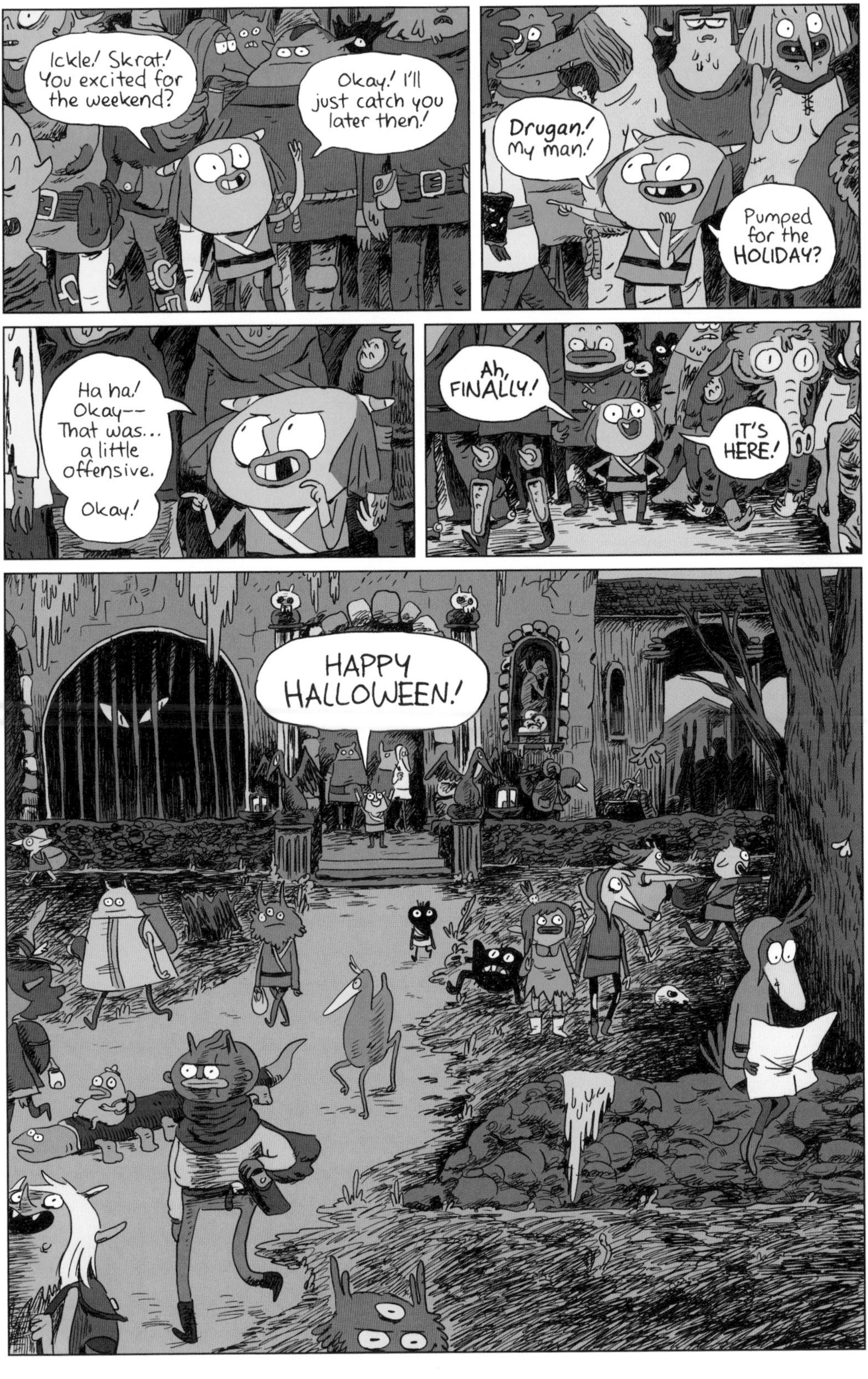
Ickle! Skrat! You excited for the weekend?
Okay! I'll just catch you later then!
Drugan! My man!
Pumped for the HOLIDAY?
Ha ha! Okay-- That was... a little offensive. Okay!
Ah, FINALLY!
IT'S HERE!
HAPPY HALLOWEEN!

Isn't today just wonderful?

Hey, Klem.

Can't you just **feel** it in the air?

Hm?

The MAGIC! *The Halloween MAGIC!* It's wonderful!

But we don't even celebrate Halloween.

It's a human holiday.

CANDY SHORTAGE HITS REPUGIA!

SWEETS SHORTAGE LEAVES LOCAL RESIDENTS SOUR

And even if we did, you've seen the papers.

What good is Halloween without any candy?

10 WAYS TO ENGORGE YOUR ABDOMEN FOR SUMMER

BY AB. MUNGO

GYM RENO

Oh, Sellie! My dear, sweet, little Sellie!

What happened to you? To your sense of wonder! Of romance!

Imagine the crackle of dead leaves beneath your boot heels--

The warm glow of a gutted-out pumpkin--

The haunting wail of a ghost seeking its vengeance--

A ghost cursed to walk the earth until...until—

You get the idea.

Halloween is a day anything can happen...

Oh, no!

Verena Snout?! You're not serious! She's one of the COOL KIDS!

AND WHAT'RE WE?!

Frhends! 'Eez rocksh thayst shorta 'ike cayndshee!

He said the same thing about pine cones an hour ago.

MUNCH MUNCH

ow

ow

MUNCH MUNCH

ow

mu m

Pfft!

I don't care what you say!

I'm going over there!

Klem! Wait!

Hee hee! WHAT?! Seriously?

Yeah, her das some sort eneral or who

—oh there's no way she with all that

Ahem!

she said that! Doesn't she know that Scuzz is wi Grundina now?

It's he idea Scuzz e likes.

hat's sane. literall cray

Ahem!

No way. Grun way

Yeah, and they ll just stopped and looked at him like "Do you mind?"

has big umb.

ho is taking lance? out her fling?

What else uld she do e stopped

whatever

ight as call it and be th it

You mig well just a night one

Hehe That, grody believ still ha Serio

That's n even th

Plus, there's e party tonig and if she

A PARTY SOUNDS LIKE FUN!

So, is it like a...uhm, costume thing?

It's more like a NO DORKS THING!

Ophirion! C'mon, lay off him!

Can't you see he's harmless?

What did you WANT, anyway?

I just thought maybe...

What? That you could hang with us?

I think those kids are more your speed!

It's not a "mystery"! Your teeth hurt because you've been eating rocks and pine cones all day!

You're right.

I just thought maybe--

You'd want some of my CANDY.

Wait! Did you say "candy"? Oh, yeah!

I have ALL kinds of candy. Crud™, Gloop™, Fizzy Fruit™, everything. It's just too bad I don't have anybody special to share it with... you know!

WOW! You should bring it to the party tonight! Isn't that right, Ophirion?

Hm. Maybe you're right. Yeah, you can come to the party. Really?

OKAY! I'll see ya then! WAIT!

Remember this, dork, and remember it well... I DON'T like to be disappointed.

Either I'll be eating candy tonight or you'll be eating a mouthful of broken teeth.

Got it?

Check-aroonie!

See ya tonight, dork! BWAHAHA-- henh henh!

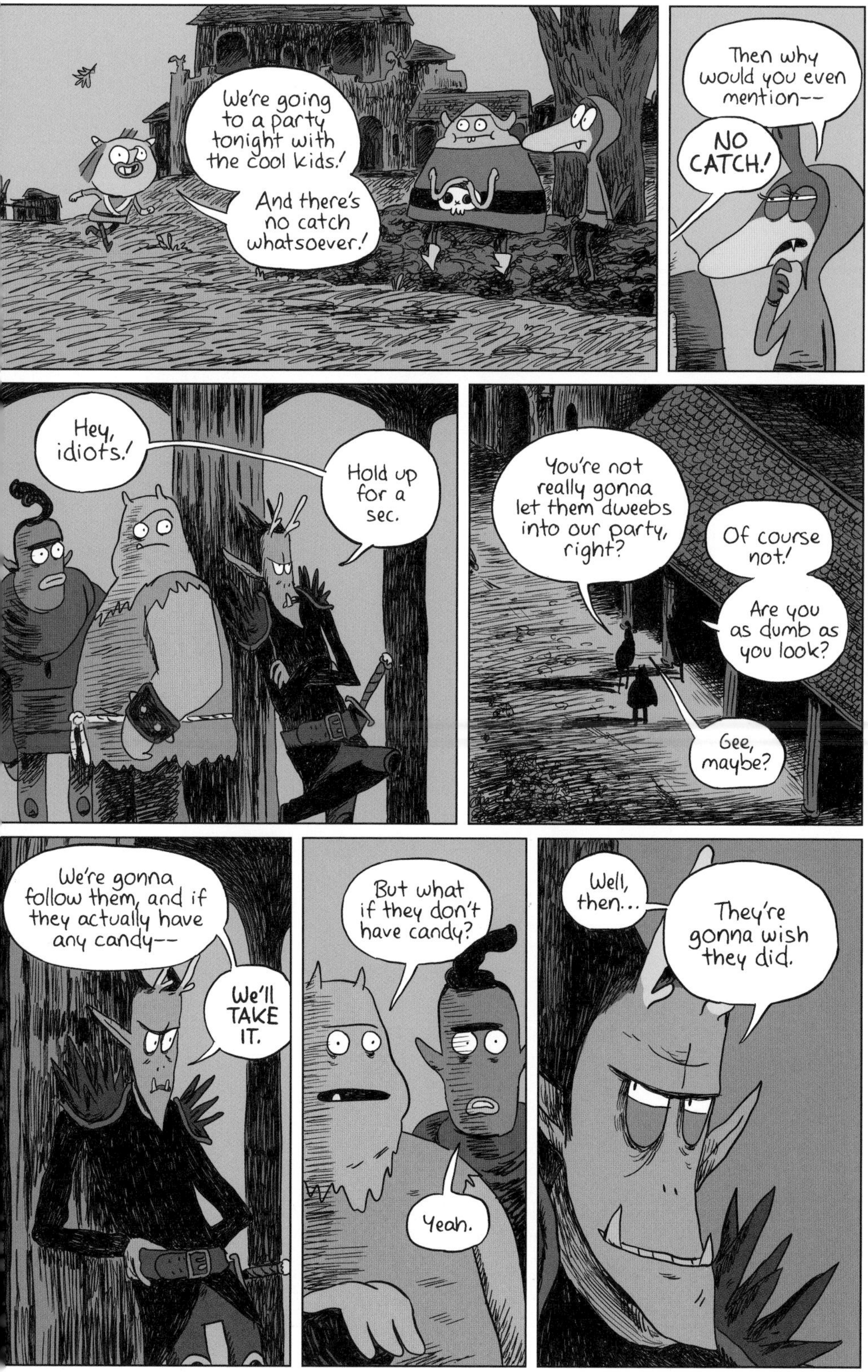
We're going to a party tonight with the cool kids!
And there's no catch whatsoever!
Then why would you even mention--
NO CATCH!
Hey, idiots!
Hold up for a sec.
You're not really gonna let them dweebs into our party, right?
Of course not!
Are you as dumb as you look?
Gee, maybe?
We're gonna follow them, and if they actually have any candy--
We'll TAKE IT.
But what if they don't have candy?
Yeah.
Well, then...
They're gonna wish they did.

Okay, it should be just over this hill.

Where are we?

You said we just needed to pick up a few small things for the party.

And in a way, I didn't technically lie--

I think it's important to remember that.

Especially for the next ten seconds.

NO!

NO NO NO NO NO NO

Wait! Just hear me out!

NO!

It's just a quick trip!

To the HUMAN WORLD!

You have no idea what it's like over there!

From the stories I've heard from my dad, humans are terrible!

They have tiny little white teeth and rub things on their bodies that smell like flowers!

Those are just STORIES! Humans are harmless!

Oh, you're a human expert, I guess?

No! I'm just sayin'!

Also, we know nothing about how portals really work! It's too dangerous!

KRZZK!

We could end up anywhere! You'd have to be an idiot to just jump in--

KRZZZT!

POP!

UGH! FINE! Let's go!

But I'm ONLY GOING to find Brolo! I'm not staying to look for candy!

THUD!

And this doesn't mean that I'm not still mad at you.

I don't know why you want to impress those jerks.

Also, Verena is not interested in you. As a matter of fact she barely knows that--

Heeeeeyyyyyyyyyyyyy

SHOVE!

KRZZZT!

Hup!

KRZZZT!

A PORTAL TO THE HUMAN WORLD!

So that's how he plans to get his candy!

Very clever, dork.

RUSTLE RUSTLE RUSTLE

And not JUST clever, but brave.

He's a true Repugian. Brave, clever, willing to steal from the humans--

I'd respect him if he weren't such a spineless dork.

That's very confusing.

Come on! We have to follow them!

We need that candy!

But, uh--

He's bringing the candy to the party, right?

Couldn't we wait to steal it then and save ourselves the trouble?

I will not have my candy sullied with the taste of dork triumph.

KRZZZZT

The weird part is...that really resonated with me.

KRZZT!

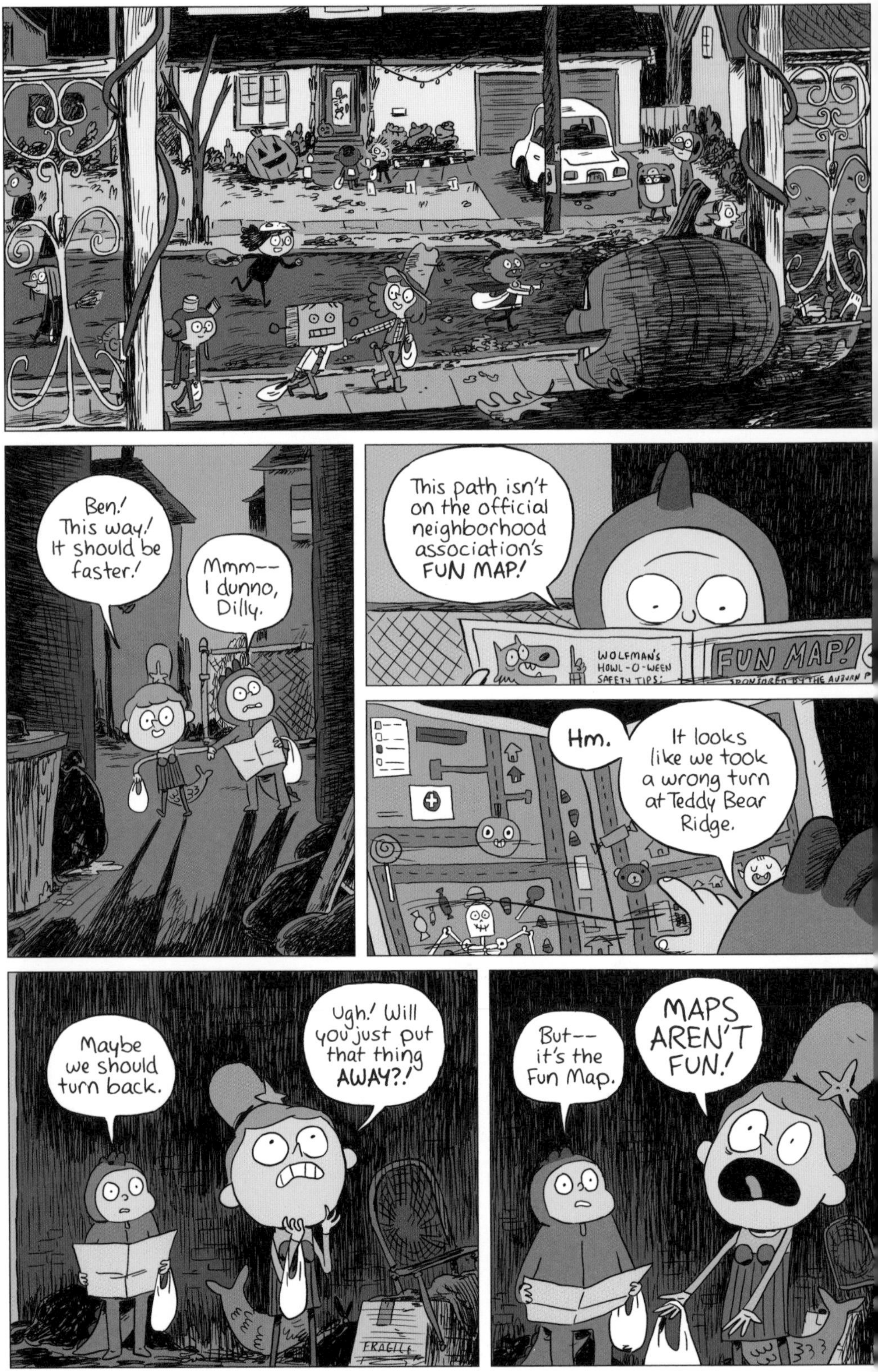
Ben! This way! It should be faster!
Mmm-- I dunno, Dilly.
This path isn't on the official neighborhood association's FUN MAP!
WOLFMAN'S HOWL-O-WEEN SAFETY TIPS:
FUN MAP!
Hm.
It looks like we took a wrong turn at Teddy Bear Ridge.
Maybe we should turn back.
Ugh! Will you just put that thing AWAY?!
FRAGILE
But-- it's the Fun Map.
MAPS AREN'T FUN!

I suppose you know a better way to minimize risk **and** maximize fun?

What risk?

Nothing dangerous ever happens in Auburn Pines!

Well, now—

I dunno if I'd say THAT!

KRZzZT!

Oof!

Argh!

BROOOOLO!

Brolo! Bro-lo!

Brolo!

Well, we tried. Now gimme a boost.

What?!

I'm going back through the portal.

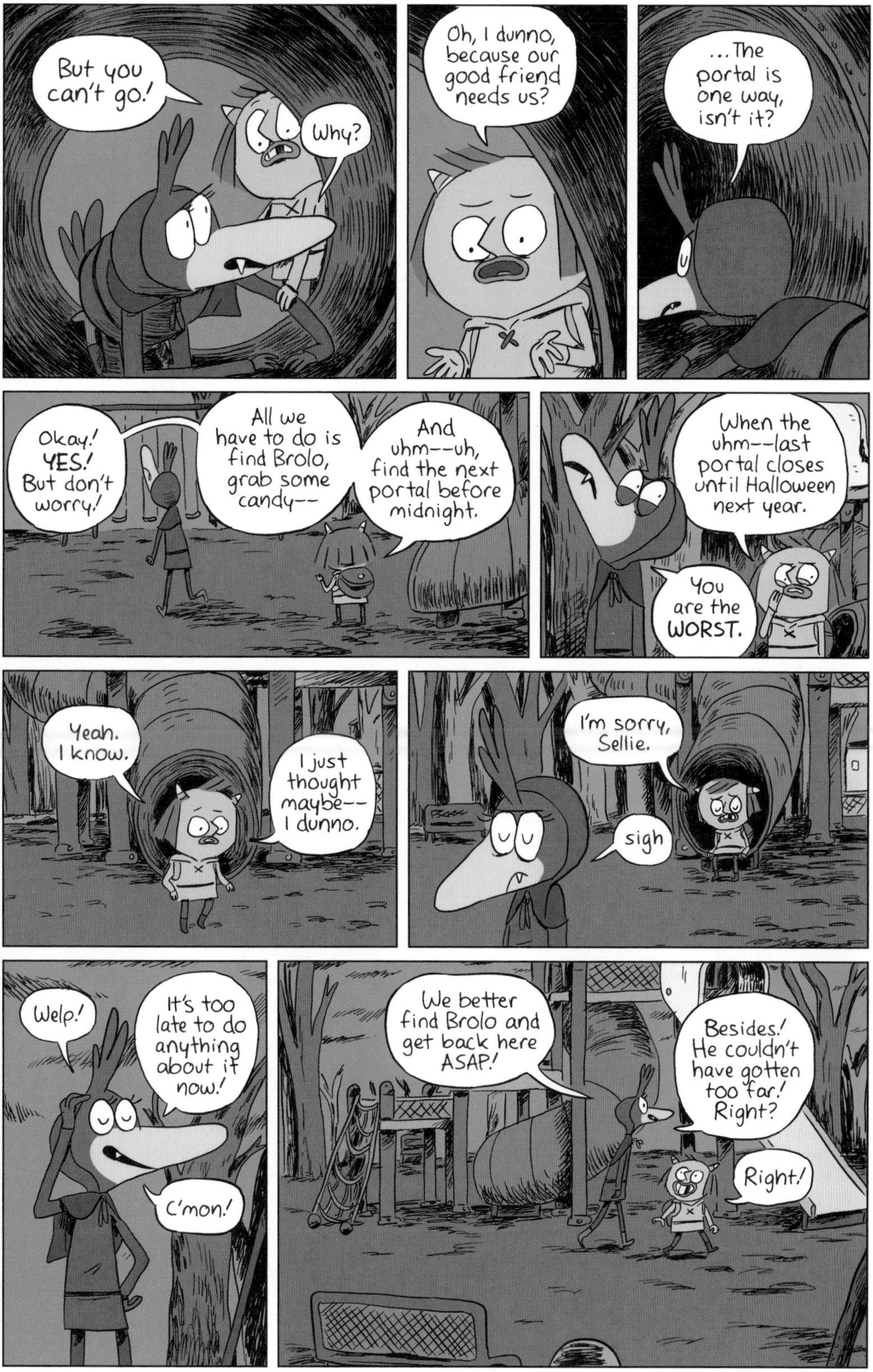

But you can't go!
Why?
Oh, I dunno, because our good friend needs us?
...The portal is one way, isn't it?
Okay! YES! But don't worry!
All we have to do is find Brolo, grab some candy--
And uhm--uh, find the next portal before midnight.
When the uhm--last portal closes until Halloween next year.
You are the WORST.
Yeah. I know.
I just thought maybe-- I dunno.
I'm sorry, Sellie.
sigh
Welp!
It's too late to do anything about it now!
C'mon!
We better find Brolo and get back here ASAP!
Besides! He couldn't have gotten too far! Right?
Right!

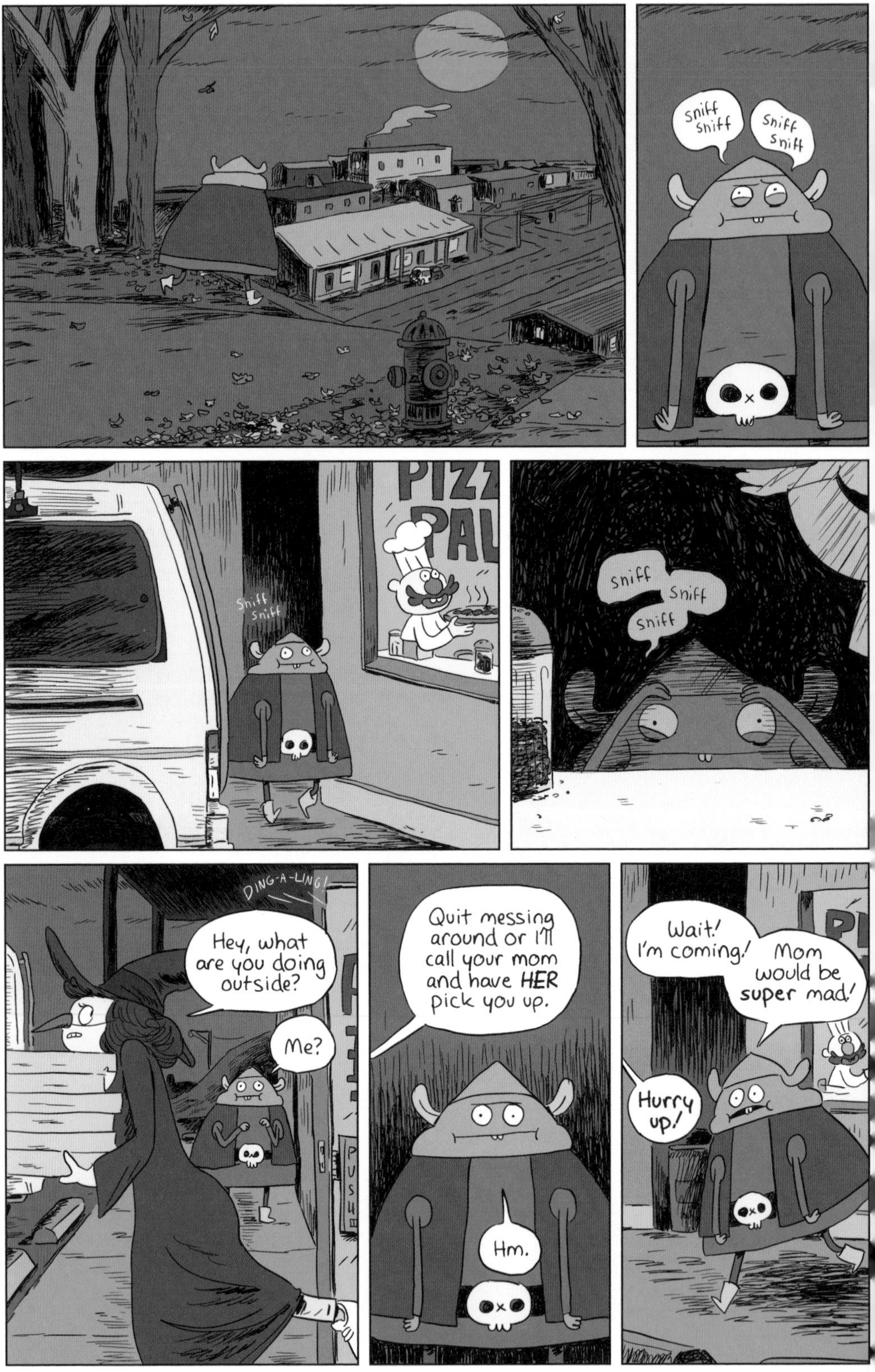

sniff sniff
Sniff sniff
Sniff sniff
PIZZ
PAL
sniff
Sniff
sniff
DING-A-LING!
Hey, what are you doing outside?
Me?
PUSH
Quit messing around or I'll call your mom and have HER pick you up.
Hm.
Wait! I'm coming!
Mom would be super mad!
Hurry up!

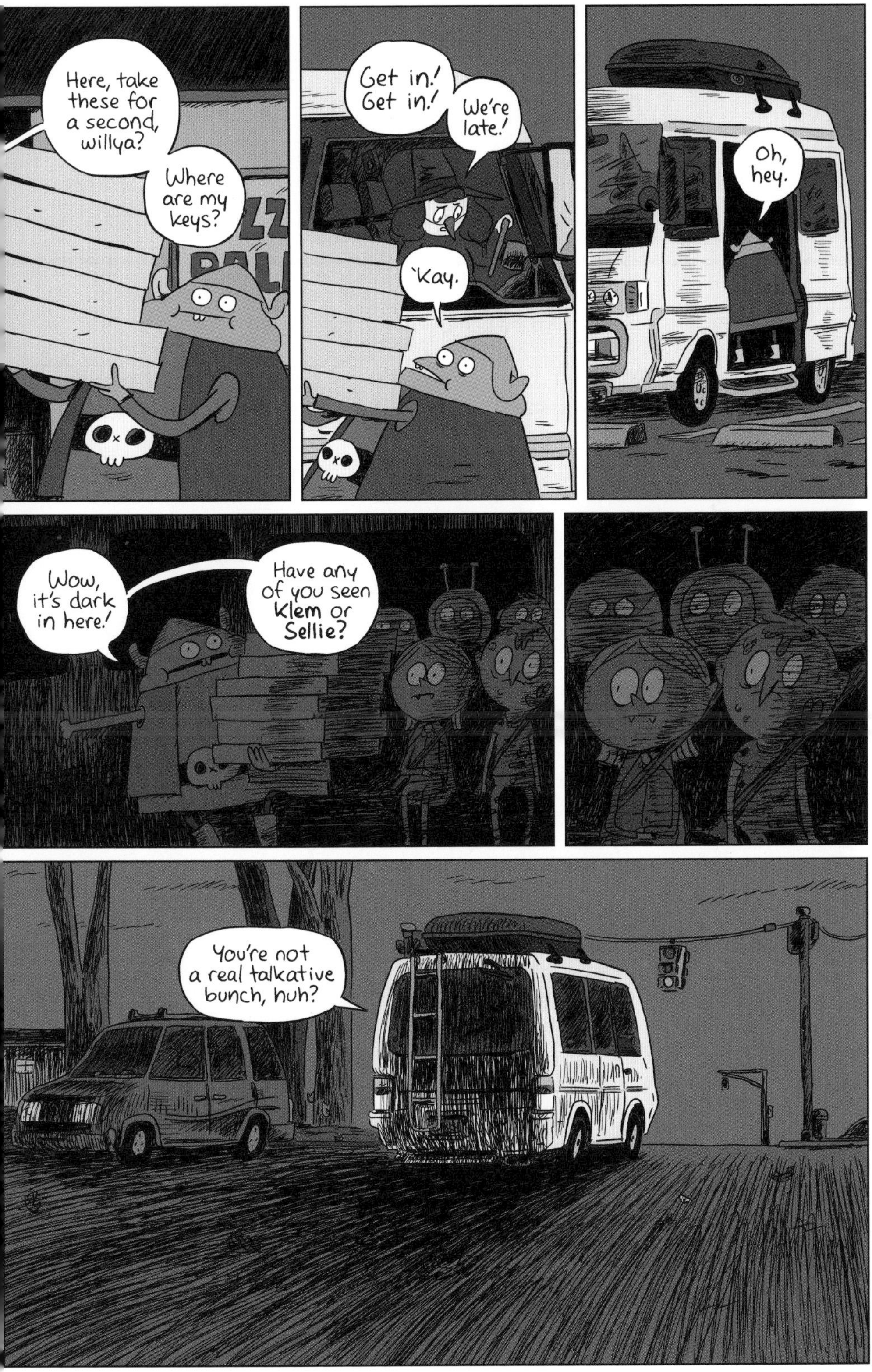
Here, take these for a second, willya?
Where are my keys?
Get in! Get in!
We're late!
`Kay.
Oh, hey.
Wow, it's dark in here!
Have any of you seen **Klem** or **Sellie**?
You're not a real talkative bunch, huh?

All of our candy! Gone! It's ruined!

Halloween is ruined!

Aw!

They even took the FUN MAP!

Why?

We shoulda fought those jerks!

Are you kidding? They were three times our size!

Yeah, but...

It was MY candy.

WAIT!

Just a sec...

Here! I stashed some candy in my underwear!

Aw, Ben!

That's so sweet...and also makes me want to throw up a little.

KRRZzZzT!

Hey! Dorks! Is that candy?

Oh, come on!

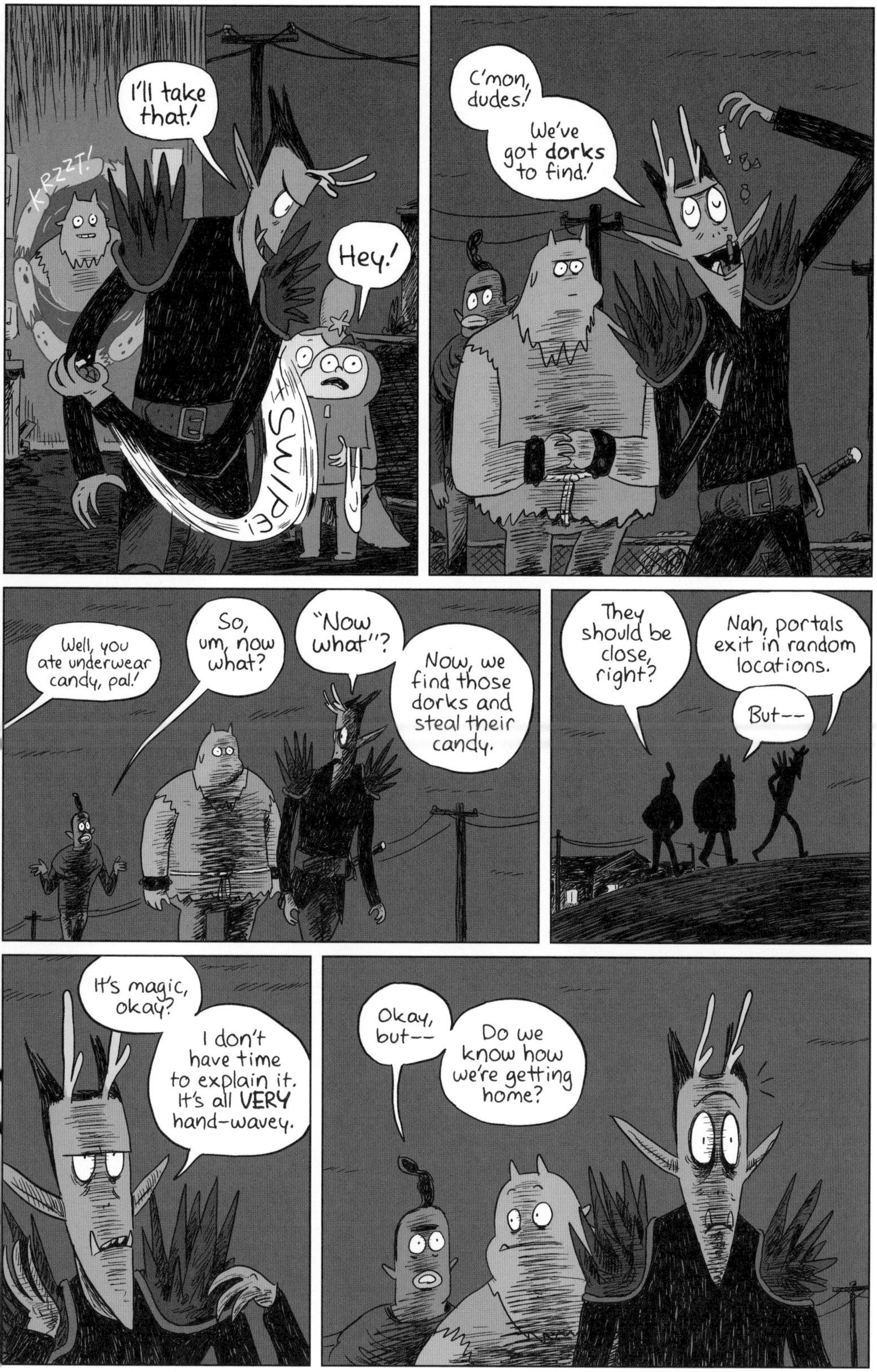
KRZZT!
I'll take that!
Hey!
SWIPE!
C'mon, dudes!
We've got **dorks** to find!
Well, you ate underwear candy, pal!
So, um, now what?
"Now what"?
Now, we find those dorks and steal their candy.
They should be close, right?
Nah, portals exit in random locations.
But--
It's magic, okay?
I don't have time to explain it. It's all **VERY** hand-wavey.
Okay, but--
Do we know how we're getting home?

I hope we get home in time for the party...

C'mon! What's so special about Verena Snout?

Uhm, maybe that her skin is like a greasy rag used to clean the bottom of a wheelbarrow?

Or maybe that she smells like mung beans and old milk left out in the sun?

Hmpf!

Or maybe that her hair is like a braid of snails that, uhm--that--

That--

Holy cow.

Halloween! Actual human Halloween!

Full of actual humans?

BoYOhBoYOhBoYOh...OhBoYOhBoYOhBoY

Wait! It could be a trap!

What if they realize we're not human?

They won't!

WOW! They carve their pumpkins just like I'd heard!

I dunno about this, Klem--

We should get outta here.

Are you kidding?

This is paradise! Look around!

The candy flows like water!

Monsters rule the night!

Can't you feel it, Sellie? This is it!

The Halloween magic!

Can't you smell it?

I think your nose is overly sensitive.

The smell of cider and candy! It sends a tingle down my spine!

It's like my whole body is awake, energy oozing from every pore!

Anything can happen on Halloween!

The dead can rise! Humans and monsters can walk side by side!

Don't you LOVE IT, Sellie?!

It's kinda cool, I guess.

Hey! Can we stop at a few houses really quick?

We have time! Check it out!

Hm.

See?

This map shows the locations of portals between our worlds and when they usually show up!

Usually?

Well, I guess it looks like we have time...

Where'd you get this?

Wouldn't YOU like to know!

New plan, first we steal that map, then we steal the CANDY!

Does the order matter?

I'm only askin' cuz the way you said it made it sound like the order matters.

It was for dramatic effect!

Just a few houses, right?

Ooooh! That one is handing out Slime Beetles™! They're Verena's favorite!

They're my favorite, TOO...

Yay!

Thunk!

We're here!

Who's ready to party?

YAY!

Phew!

Uh-oh.

Can you believe they were giving away full-size Crud™ bars? They're HUGE!

I'm gonna eat until I barf!

Amazing.

See? I knew you'd have a good time.!

Yeah, yeah.

Don't gloat.

It's ugly.

It's getting late anyway. We better find Brolo before the last portal closes.

It looks like we're not too far from the next one at least.

HEY.! Let's take the shortcut through this dark alley.!

WOOOOOOOOOOO....

WOOOOOOOOOOOO

Sure.

Hm.

There sure are a lot of candy wrappers on the ground here.

Weird, huh?

I'm starting to have second thoughts about this alley--

Hey!

Cool! It's a map of the neighborhood!

Boy, would this have been handy a few hours ago!

Sellie! Check this out!

Sellie?

Uh--

Now might not be the best time...

Listen! I don't know what you've heard, but—

We are NORMAL HUMAN CHILDREN!

4-yeah! So, if you don't mind, I need to go home and BRUSH MY TINY HUMAN-CHILD TEETH WITH MINTY PASTE!

Yeah, I'll say!

I've been so busy ENJOYING THE DAYLIGHT and EATING THINGS OTHER THAN RATS, I almost forgot the TEETH BRUSHING ACTIVITY myself!

Gimme your candy, dorks!

Ophirion?

What'd you call me?

Sorry! You just remind me of someone!

Candy! Now!

Psst! Sellie! What are we gonna do?

Sellie?

You might have to dig a bit. The really good stuff is buried at the bottom.

Thanks.

Sellie!

Time's up, dork!

Gimme the candy now or ELSE!

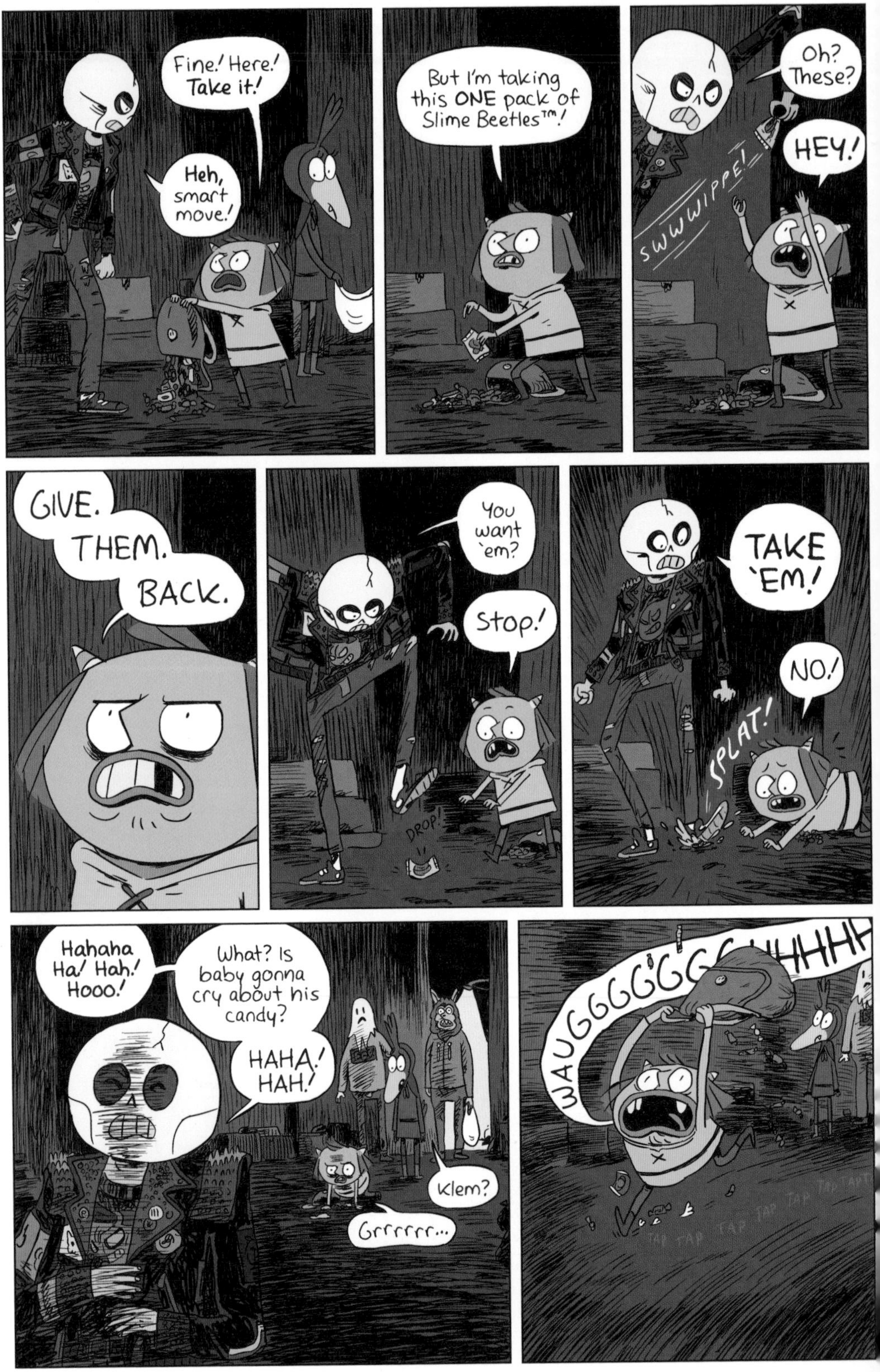
Fine! Here! Take it!
Heh, smart move!
But I'm taking this ONE pack of Slime Beetles™!
Oh? These?
SWWWIPPE!
HEY!
GIVE. THEM. BACK.
You want 'em?
Stop!
DROP!
TAKE 'EM!
NO!
SPLAT!
Hahaha Ha! Hah! Hooo!
What? Is baby gonna cry about his candy?
HAHA! HAH!
Klem?
Grrrrrr...
WAUGGGGGGGHHHH
TAP TAP TAP TAP TAP TAP TAP

BWANGO!

BFWWOOOSH

AHHH.!!

Goo?

Forget this!

Huff Huff Huff Huff

You okay?

He ruined everything.

Hey, don't worry about it.

Those guys dropped the candy. We've got plenty of stuff!

And--

And look, I'm sure Verena will understand about the Slime Beetles™.

They weren't for Verena--

They were for you.

I know they're your favorite.

I know you're mad at me for dragging you along.

I super am.

I know.

I thought maybe you'd forgive me if--

I dunno. Sellie, you're such a good friend and--

Klem?

Yeah.

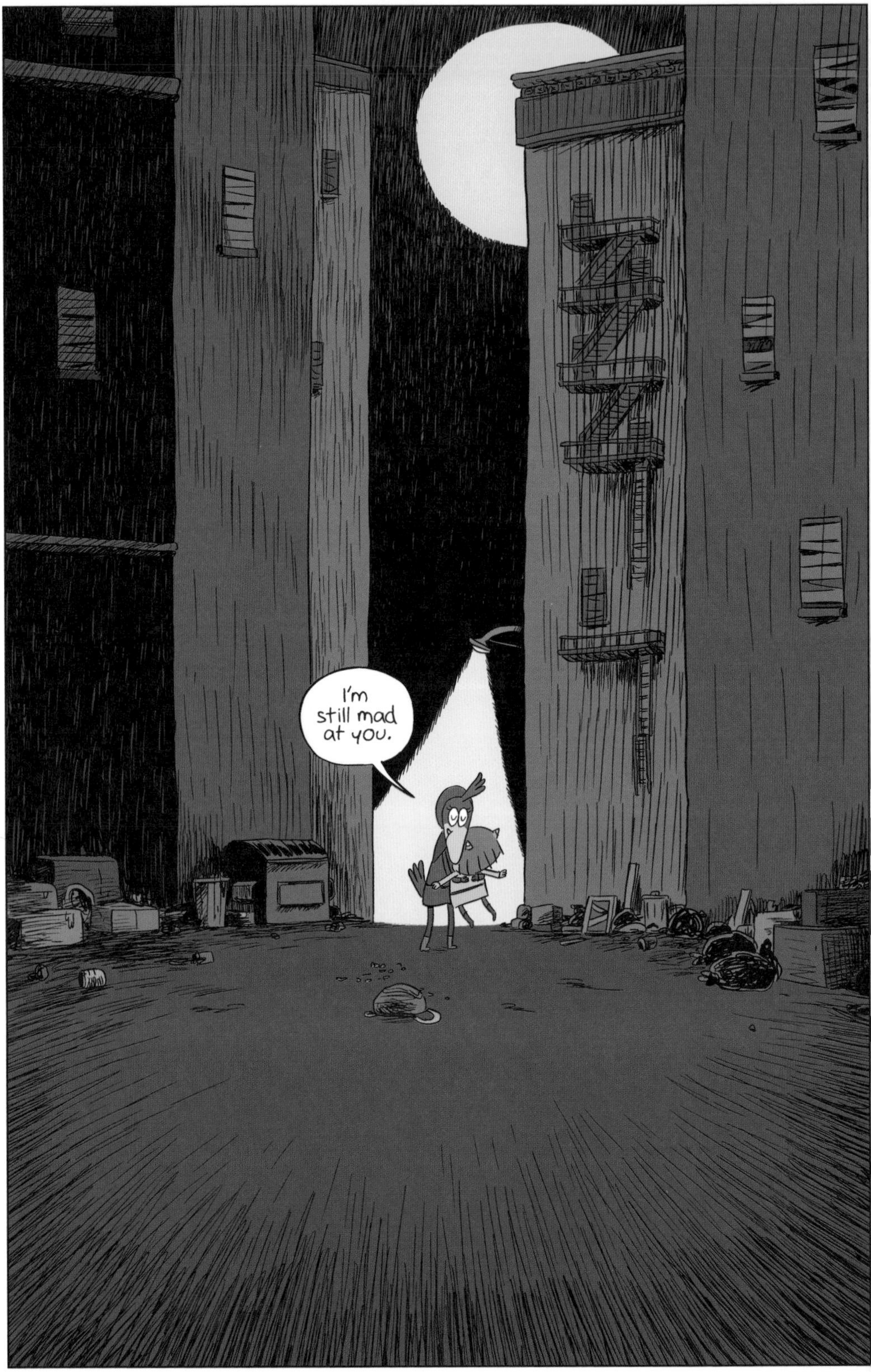
I'm still mad at you.

What are you supposed to be?

Bunny?

Too ugly.

Tree Sloth?

Still too ugly.

Armadillo?

Getting warmer...

Manitee.

Oh, yeah! That's it! Like a sick manitee!

Actually, he's a **trowbog!**

GULP!

And he has exactly ten seconds to explain what he's doing at our party!

Or ELSE!

Well, I guess this is it.

There's only a few minutes until the last portal home, and Brolo is nowhere to be seen.

I'm a terrible friend.

No, you're not!

It's not your fault he wandered off! Besides--

I actually had a really great time tonight!

D'aw!

Isn't that cute!

Ophirion!

Did'ja miss me?

First things first!

I came all this way to make sure I get my candy!

So, boys!

Please do the honors!

HEY! That's ours!

Wait, I thought the map thing went first...

Shh!

Now that that bit of dirty business is done, it's time for the good news!

You did it, buddy!

Hey!

Uh.

D-did what?

"DID WHAT"?

Did you forget why you came here?!

Why you risked life and limb?!

Oof!

BONK!

Oof!

You're one of the COOL KIDS now!

Just wait'll I tell Verena about how you came all the way to the HUMAN WORLD, just to get her candy!

She loves brave dudes, you know?

Really?

Aww, yeah.

Just one more thing-- Ditch your loser friends behind here.

What?

I don't want them getting their losery stink on me.

Wait! But the next portal isn't coming until next Halloween!

You can't!

Hm. Lemme rephrase this cuz I'm afraid there's been a little bit of a misunderstanding.

You can come with me––

Or you can stay here with them!

Either way––

I'm taking THE MAP!

So, dork––

What'll it be? Stay here with your loser friends, or come back and party with the––

Oh, definitely my friends. Of course.

I mean, obviously.

You guys are total dinguses.

The weird part is you still thought it was a hard choice––

That's very telling.

WHAT?!

That's not how this was supposed to happen!

Arrrgh!

Forget this! Forget you!

I'm taking your stupid map!

Good luck getting home with the power of friendship!

Or what the donk ever!

Well, that could've gone better.

I don't know how.

But they took our map!

You mean THIS map?

How?

There's no time to explain! The last portal closes in ten minutes!

But you just had time to say that!

No time!

Ha ha! Come on!

How'd you do it?

Let's just put it this way... they got A map!

Uh, Ophirion? This don't look right to me.

Oh, really? I suppose I better call Abraham Ortelius and let him know he can quit his day job.

None of this makes any sense!

Uh, bro?

What do these symbols even mean?!

Bro?

And just where the donk is the donkin' Li-BOO-rary?!

BRO!

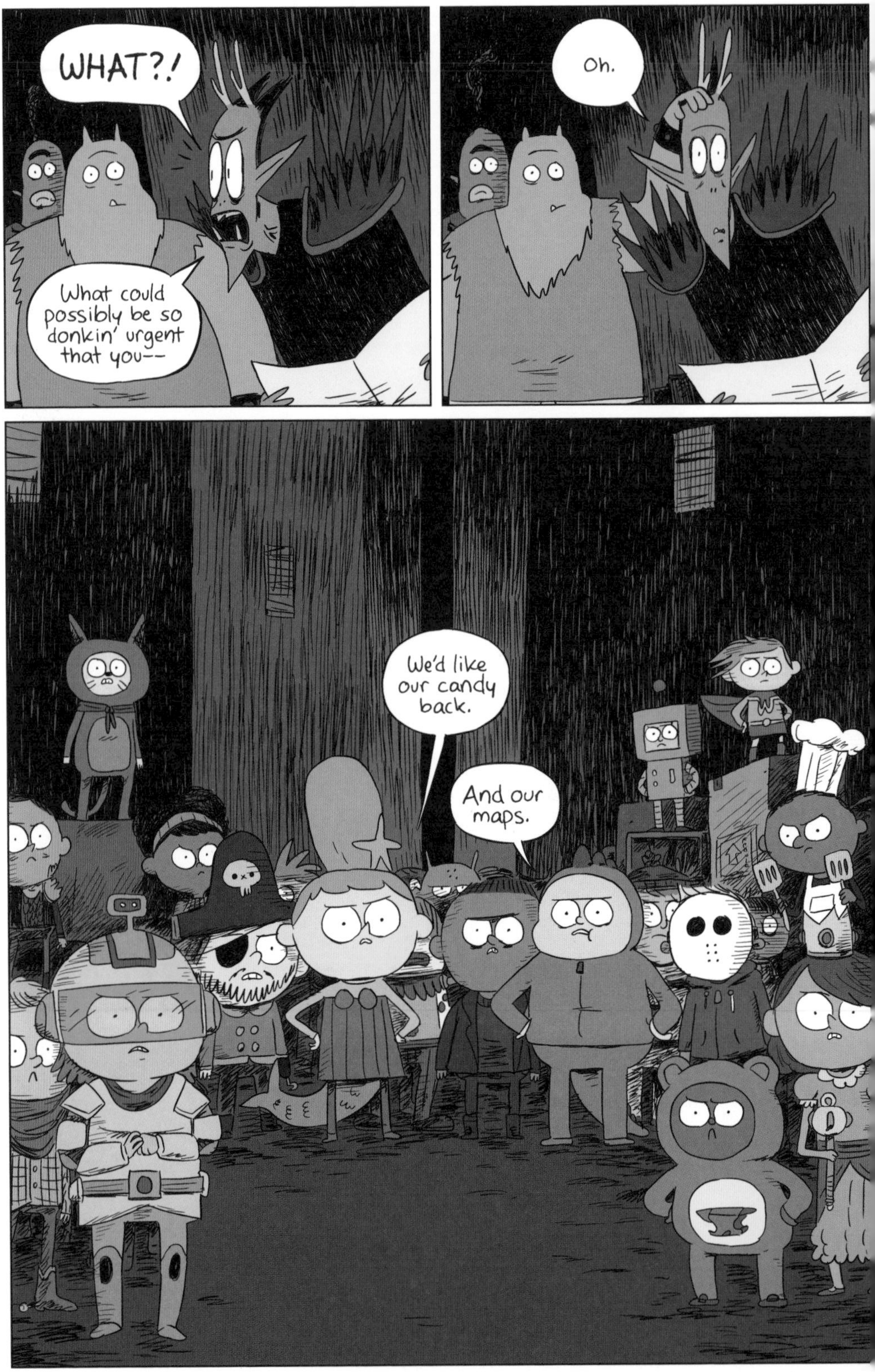
WHAT?!
What could possibly be so donkin' urgent that you--
Oh.
We'd like our candy back.
And our maps.

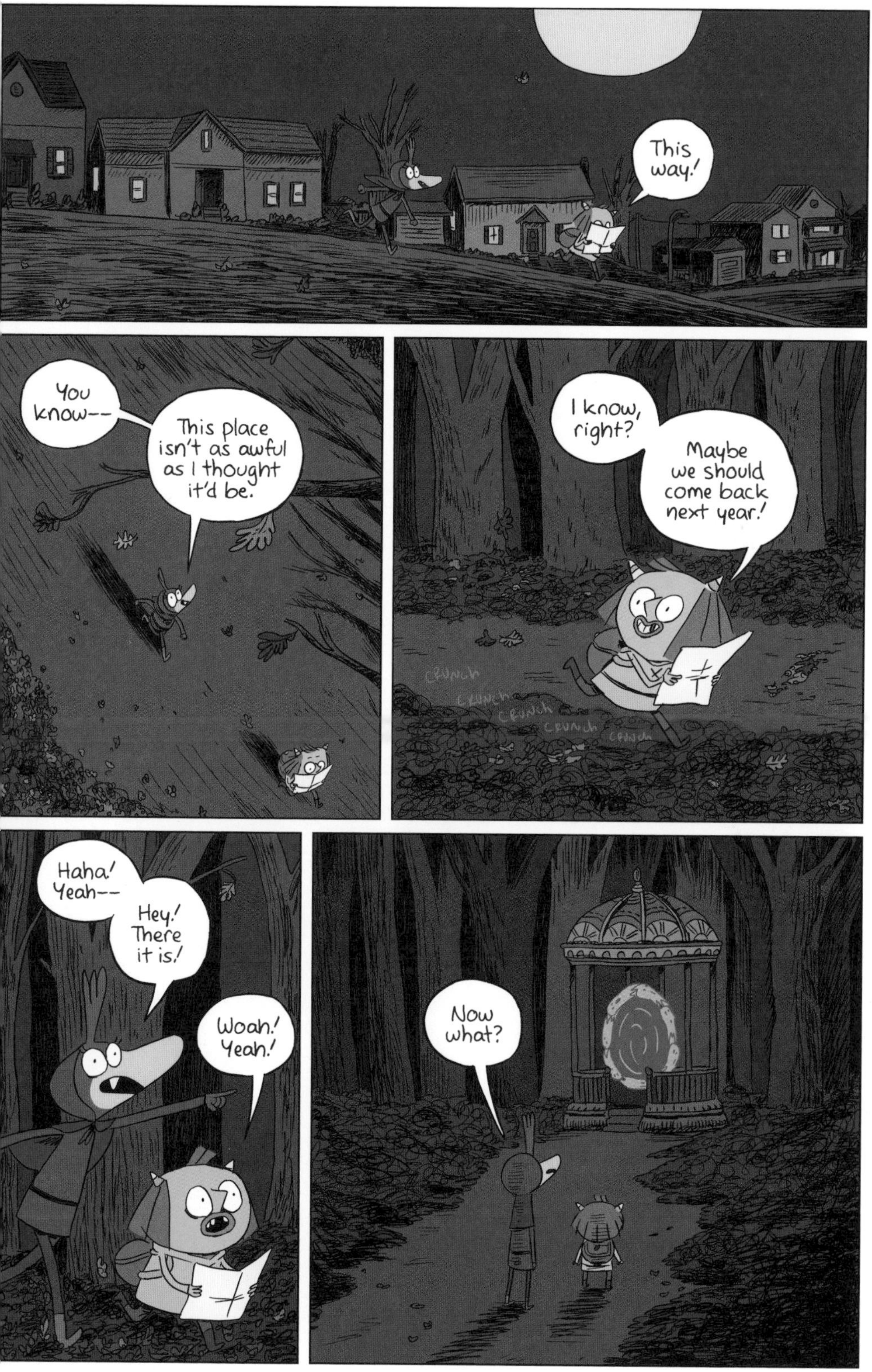
This way!
You know--
This place isn't as awful as I thought it'd be.
I know, right?
Maybe we should come back next year!
CRUNCH
CRUNCH
CRUNCH
CRUNCH
CRUNCH
Haha! Yeah--
Hey! There it is!
Woah! Yeah!
Now what?

We can't leave Brolo here by himself for a whole year.

I know.

Which is why I'm staying.

What? No!

Don't be stupid!

One of us has to stay to find Brolo, the other person should go back to get help.

I got us into this mess, so--

I'm sorry.

Sellie, please. It's the only way.

No way!

How selfish ARE you?

I'm not gonna let you martyr yourself just to feel better.

I like you too much to go a year without you.

Besides, you owe me too much for screwing up to argue.

I'm staying.

Sellie--

VVRRRrrrrrrrrrrrrre

HONK HONK HONK

What the?

SKREEEECH!

FWOOOOOOOSSSH!

Thunk!

Hi.

BROLO!

Brolo! How'd you find us?

Allow me to explain! I'm Lucy and this is Everett!

Last Halloween we thwarted a Repugian invasion that nearly--

LUCY!

Have fun with your friends, I'll be back to pick you up in half an hour!

Yeah, Mom?

Okay, Mom!

Where was I?

Oh, yes!

Part of our adventure took us to your homeland of Repugia!

I'm sorry.

Don't be!

It was fascinating! And more pertinently--

While I was there, I began to scribble down my hypothesis concerning portal generation.

Which I believe you're holding!

The map!

You drew this?

Actually, I did.

Wow! Even all these cool dragons in the margin?

You like them?

Of course! But I'm a little confused...

What do all the "E+L's" with the hearts stand for?

Okay, maybe we're done with the map.

I suppose you want this back now.

Please, keep it!

Really?

You never know when you might want to visit!

Gee! Thanks!

Plus, it's not very precise.

We'd better get going before the portal closes.

Thanks again! For everything!

Wait! There's one more thing!

Brolo told me about the candy shortage in Repugia and how much you love Halloween--

So... I wanted you to have this.

NO WAY! SERIOUSLY?!

Yeah, It's n--

Thank you!

So long! We'll see you next year!

If Wren or Reynold ask, I'm saying you invited them.

Wait-- what?

KRRRZT!

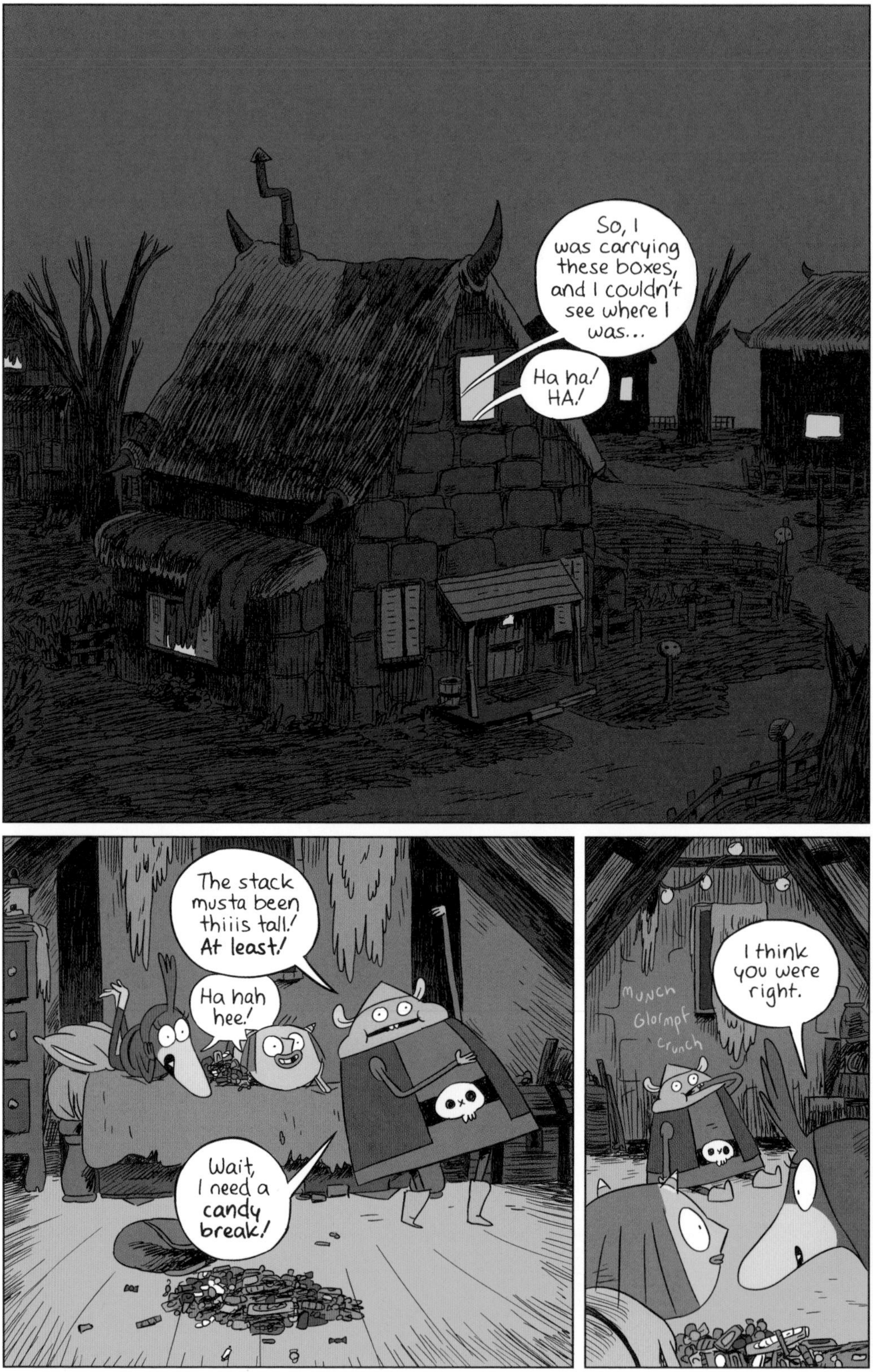
So, I was carrying these boxes, and I couldn't see where I was...
Ha ha! HA!
The stack musta been thiiis tall! At least!
Ha hah hee!
Wait, I need a candy break!
munch
Glormpf
crunch
I think you were right.

I can feel it.

I can feel the magic. The Halloween magic--

That spark in the air!

The smell of dried leaves!

It's like a current of energy running through my whole body!

See? I told you!

Anything can happen on Halloween!

Yeah. You're right--

It sure can.

Okay! Break's over!

So, there I was with the boxes--

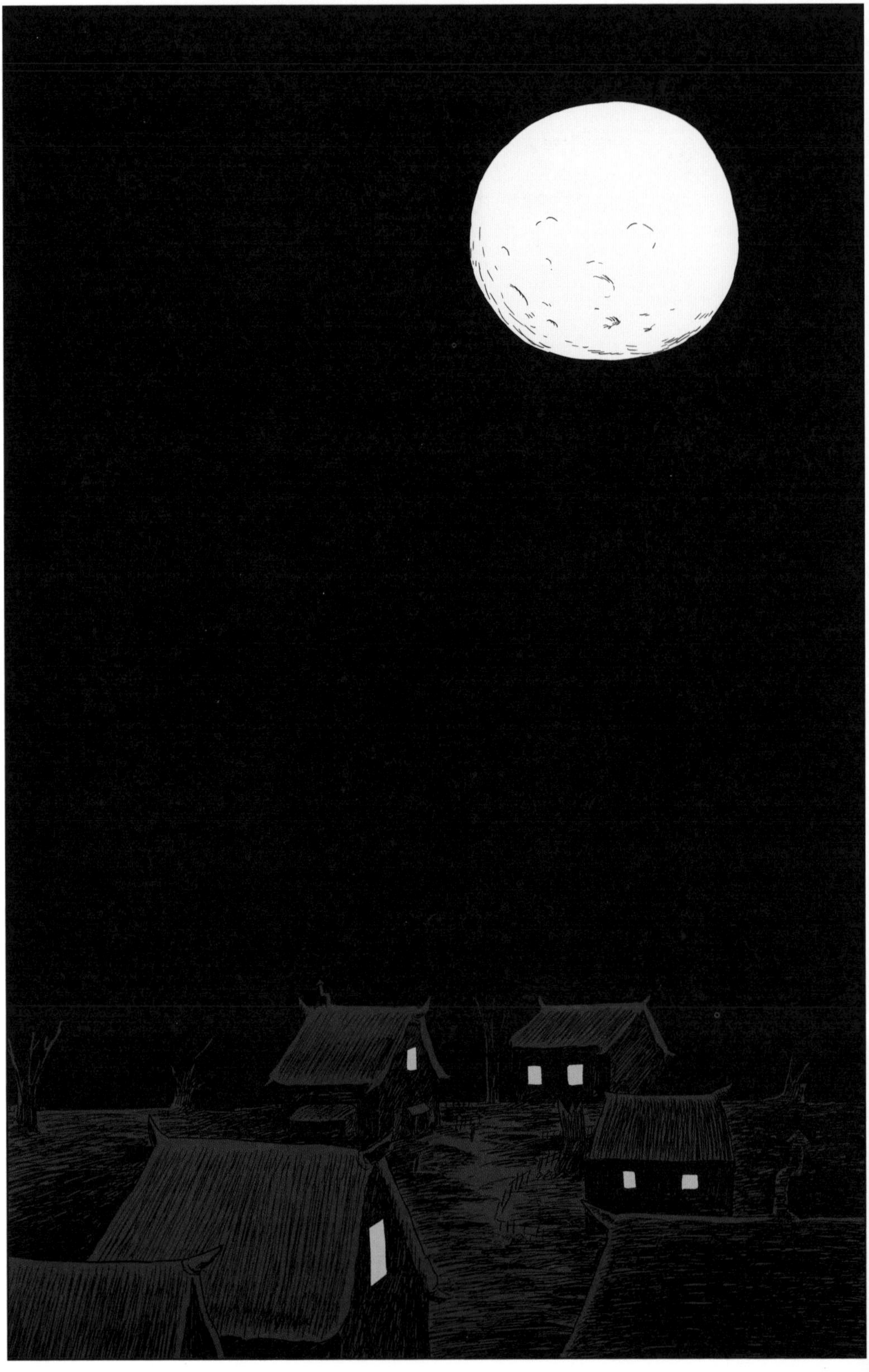

AFTERWORD

By
TASHA SOUNART

HALLOWEEN has always been my favorite holiday. Not because of the scary parts (I was always more on the trembly side) but because of the creativity behind it. Halloween is the one day of the year when everyone can run around as whatever they want to be, whether it's something scary, cute, powerful, or funny. People allow themselves to try on new personas that could be completely different from how they are in everyday life.

As a child, I always thought the setting of Halloween would make a very cool game. There were just so many things I loved about it—the exploration of the darkened neighborhood with a pack of friends, the brightly lit pumpkins on all the doorsteps, the slight smell of smoke coming from the chimneys, the crunch of fallen leaves underfoot. Oh, and there was always the intense candy trading session that followed. For the entire year afterward, I would carefully ration out my candy so it would last me until the next Halloween. Of course I would have to hide it from my sister, who would go through her candy in a couple of days. Sometime around the age of 11, after I had received my beloved NES, I remember drawing a group of little pixelated characters trick-or-treating. Years later, at Double Fine, I got the opportunity to actually see my idea come to life, which was simultaneously stressful and awesome.

During the project, a few things were very important to me: I wanted to keep the tone of the game funny, warm, family-friendly, and sincere—much like the Peanuts specials I loved while growing up. I wanted parents to be able to play the game along with their children, since this was the type of game I would have loved to play as a kid.

I also wanted the game to emphasize the contrast between the kids' more mundane, "normal" suburban lives, and the epic, powerful world of their imaginations. My mom would hand-make the costumes for my sister and I, so I wanted to include that crafting aspect in the game—the transformation of ordinary objects into costume pieces. Later in life, I would continue to construct my own elaborate outfits each year, even though I never learned how to sew (the glue gun is my friend). One of my proudest moments was in my 20s, when I won a contest at work with my homemade "garden gnome sitting on a hill" costume.

Another central idea in the game was that every character (boys and girls) had the ability to wear any of the costumes. As a tomboy growing up, I was often teased for liking "boy stuff." But on Halloween, I could be whatever I wanted, whether that was a space warrior, a magician, a unicorn, or a clown. Kids have fun exploring all sorts of identities and scenarios and shouldn't have limitations placed upon their imaginations.

After *Costume Quest* was released, a single page comic based on the game started making the rounds on Twitter and made its way to Double Fine. This is how I was introduced to the quirky and charming art of Zac Gorman. (I still want a print of that comic, by the way!) Zac's art style and sense of humor mesh perfectly with the game's universe, so I can't think of a better match for the graphic novel. In this book we get to explore more of how the Repugians experience the world—what would monster children think of Halloween and trick-or-treating?

Now that I have a son of my own, I'm so excited for him to experience everything I loved about Halloween growing up and can't wait to play the games with him. It's really awesome to see the *Costume Quest* universe continue to be explored, through both the game's sequel, and Zac's own interpretation of the world and the new characters he's created.

Tasha Sounart (formerly Harris) is an animator and game designer who lives in San Francisco with her husband, son and two cats, Mr. Peterson and Snoopy. She was project lead on the game *Costume Quest*, which released in October 2010.

www.tashasquestlog.com • @tashascomic

Zac Gorman is an Eisner Award-wanting cartoonist and writer from Detroit, MI, best known for his work on beating *Super Mario Bros. 2* without the use of a Game Genie. Outside comics, he frequently works in television animation, doing storyboards and character designs for several hit shows with highly financially lucrative target demographics. He's also the author of the middle grade novel *Thisby Thestoop and the Black Mountain*.

magicalgametime.com • zacgorman.com • @zacgormania

Zac would like to thank Suzy for her love and affection, Gabe, Greg, Tim and everybody at Double Fine for their trust and encouragement, Charlie and the Oni team for all their hard work, Fangamer for their enthusiasm, and finally, Mom, Dad, Austin, Dave, Jason, and Erin for all their support along the way.

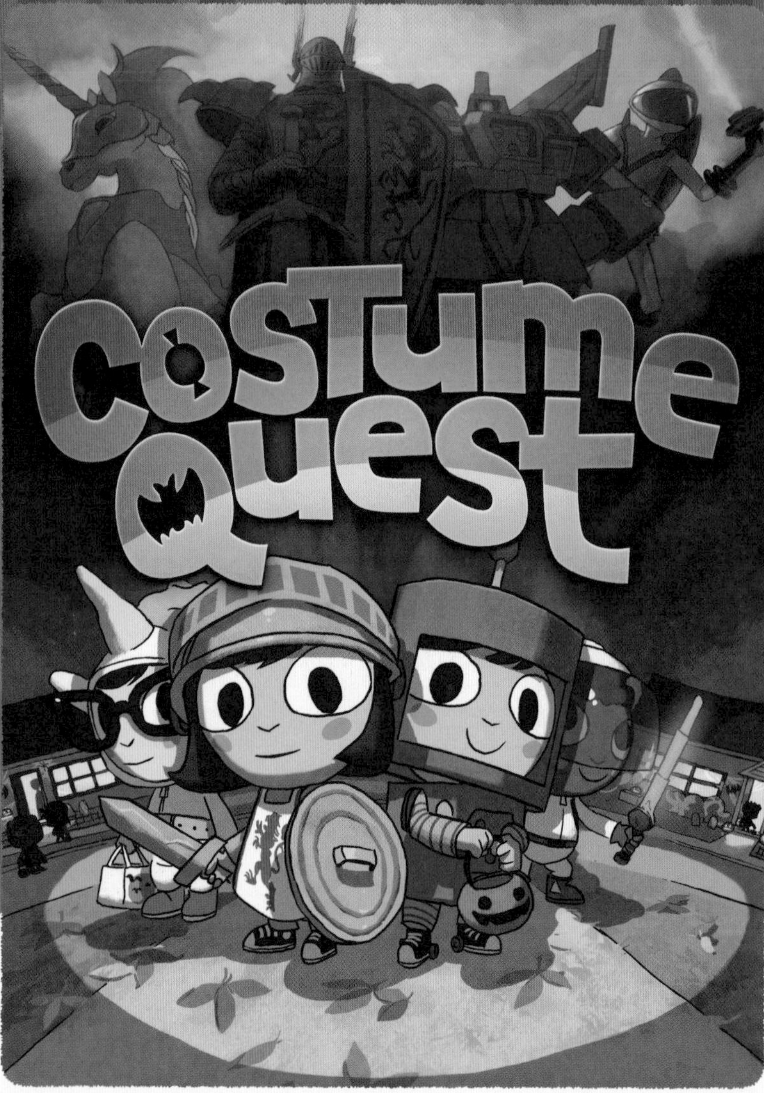
Costume Quest

BROKEN AGE

PC, Mac, Linux, iOS, Android

WWW.BROKENAGEGAME.COM

@doublefine

On Halloween,

we take our costumes off--

--and you can see us--

--as we see ourselves.

Published by Oni Press, Inc.
Joe Nozemack, founder & chief financial officer
James Lucas Jones, publisher
Charlie Chu, v.p. of creative & business development
Brad Rooks, director of operations
Melissa Meszaros, director of publicity
Margot Wood, director of sales
Sandy Tanaka, marketing design manager
Amber O'Neill, special projects manager
Troy Look, director of design & production
Hilary Thompson, senior graphic designer
Kate Z. Stone, graphic designer
Sonja Synak, junior graphic designer
Angie Knowles, digital prepress lead
Ari Yarwood, executive editor
Sarah Gaydos, editorial director of licensed publishing
Robin Herrera, senior editor
Desiree Wilson, associate editor
Alissa Sallah, administrative assistant
Jung Lee, logistics associate
Scott Sharkey, warehouse assistant

Oni Press, Inc.
1319 SE Martin Luther King Jr. Blvd.
Suite 240
Portland, OR 97214
USA

onipress.com • facebook.com/onipress • @onipress • onipress.tumblr.com

doublefine.com • @doublefine

magicalgametime.com • zacgorman.com • @zacgormania

First edition: October 2014
Softcover edition: September 2018

ISBN 978-1-62010-559-7
eISBN 978-1-62010-191-9

Library of Congress Control Number: 2018938813

10 9 8 7 6 5 4 3 2 1

PRINTED IN CHINA.

COSTUME QUEST:

INVASION OF
THE CANDY SNATCHERS

By
Zac Gorman

Based on the *Costume Quest* world created by
Tasha Sounart and Double Fine Productions

Designed by
Keith Wood

Edited by
Charlie Chu